FREE STUFF FOR KIDS

Our Pledge

We have collected and examined the best free and up-to-a-dollar offers we could find. Each supplier in this book has promised to honor properly made requests for **single items** through **1996.** Though mistakes do happen, we are doing our best to make sure this book really works.

Meadowbrook Press

Distributed by Simon & Schuster
New York

The Free Stuff Editors

Director: Bruce Lansky
Editor: David Tobey
Researcher: David Tobey
Copyeditor: Liya Lev Oertel
Production Manager: Amy Unger
Desktop Publishing Manager: Patrick Gross
Cover Design: Amy Unger

ISBN 0-88166-241-0
Simon & Schuster Ordering #: 0-671-53478-5

ISSN: 1056-9693
19th edition

Published by Meadowbrook Press, 18318 Minnetonka Boulevard, Deephaven, MN 55391.

BOOK TRADE DISTRIBUTION by Simon & Schuster, a division of Simon and Schuster, Inc., 1230 Avenue of the Americas, New York, NY 10020.

96 95   5 4 3 2 1

Printed in the United States of America

Contents

Thank You's

To Pat Blakely, Barbara Haislet, and Judith Hentges for creating and publishing the original *Rainbow Book,* proving that kids, parents, and teachers would respond enthusiastically to a source of free things by mail. They taught us the importance of carefully checking the quality of each item and doing our best to make sure that each and every request is satisfied.

Our heartfelt appreciation goes to hundreds of organizations and individuals for making this book possible. The suppliers and editors of this book have a common goal: to make it possible for kids to reach out and discover the world by themselves.

READ THIS FIRST

About This Book

Free Stuff for Kids lists hundreds of items you can send away for. The Free Stuff Editors have examined every item and think each is among the best offers available. There are no trick offers—only safe, fun, and informative things you'll like!

This book is designed for kids who can read and write. The directions on the following pages explain exactly how to request an item. Read the instructions carefully so you know how to send a request. Making sure you've filled out a request correctly is easy—just complete the *Free Stuff for Kids* Checklist on page 8. Half the fun is using the book on your own. The other half is getting a real reward for your efforts!

Each year the Free Stuff Editors create a new edition of this book, taking out old items, inserting new ones, and changing addresses and prices. It is important for you to use an updated edition because the suppliers only honor properly made requests for single items for the **current** edition. If you use this edition after **1996,** your request will not be honored.

Reading Carefully

Read the descriptions of the offers carefully to find out exactly what you're getting. Here are some guidelines to help you know what you're sending for:

• A pamphlet is usually one sheet of paper folded over and printed on both sides.

• A booklet is usually larger than a pamphlet and contains more pages, but it's smaller than a book.

Following Directions

It's important to follow each supplier's directions. On one offer, you might need to use a postcard. On another offer, you might be asked to include money or a long self-addressed, stamped envelope. If you do not follow the directions **exactly,** you might not get your request. Unless the directions tell you differently, ask for only **one** of anything you send for. Family or classroom members using the same book must send **separate** requests.

Sending Postcards

A postcard is a small card you can write on and send through the mail without an envelope. Many suppliers offering free items require you to send requests on postcards. Please do this. It saves them the time it takes to open many envelopes.

The post office sells postcards with preprinted postage. You can also buy postcards at a drugstore and put special postcard stamps on them yourself. Your local post office can tell you how much a postcard stamp currently costs. (Postcards with a picture on them are usually more expensive.) You must use a postcard that is at least 3½ by 5½ inches. (The post office will not take 3-by-5-inch index cards.) Your postcards should be addressed like the one below:

Amy Lyons
110 Deerwood
Conroe, TX 77303

The Chicago Bulls
Fan Mail
1901 West Madison
Chicago, IL 60612

Front

Dear Sir or Madam:

Please send me a Chicago Bulls fan pack. Thank you very much.

Sincerely,
Amy Lyons
110 Deerwood
Conroe, TX 77303

Back

- **Neatly print** the supplier's address on the side of the postcard that has the postage. Put your return address in the upper left-hand corner of that side as well.

- **Neatly print** your request, your name, and your address on the blank side of the postcard.

- Do not abbreviate the name of your street or city.

- Use a ballpoint pen. Pencil can be difficult to read, and ink pens often smear.

Sending Letters

Your letters should look like the one below.

- **Neatly print** the name of the item you want exactly as you see it in the directions.
- **Neatly print** your own name and address at the bottom of the letter. (Do not abbreviate the name of your street or city.)
- If you're including coins or a long self-addressed, stamped envelope, say so in the letter. And be sure to enclose the coins and the envelope!
- Put a **first-class stamp** on any envelope you send. You can get stamps at the post office.
- **Neatly print** the supplier's address in the center of the envelope and your return address in the upper left-hand corner.
- If you're sending many letters at once, make sure you put the correct letter in the correct envelope.
- Use a ballpoint pen. Pencil can be difficult to read, and ink pens often smear.

Sending a Long Self-Addressed, Stamped Envelope

If the directions say to enclose a long self-addressed, stamped envelope, here's how to do it:

• **Neatly print** your name and address in the center of a **9½-inch-long envelope** as if you were mailing it to yourself. Print your return address in the upper left-hand corner of the envelope as well. Put a **first-class stamp** on it.

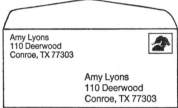

Amy Lyons
110 Deerwood
Conroe, TX 77303

Amy Lyons
110 Deerwood
Conroe, TX 77303

• **Fold up** (but don't seal!) the long self-addressed, stamped envelope, and put it inside another **9½-inch-long envelope** (along with your letter to the supplier). Put a **first-class stamp** on the second envelope, too.
• **Neatly print** the supplier's address in the center of the outside envelope and your return address in the upper left-hand corner.
• Use a ballpoint pen.

Sending Money

Many of the suppliers in this book are not charging you for their items. However, the cost of postage and handling is high today, and suppliers must charge you for this. If the directions say to enclose money, **you must do so.** Here are a few rules about sending money:

• Tape the coins to your letter so they won't break out of the envelope.
• Don't stack your coins on top of each other in the envelope.
• Don't use pennies and avoid using nickels. These coins will add weight to your envelope, and you may need to use more than one stamp.
• If an item costs $1.00, send a one-dollar bill instead of coins. Don't tape dollar bills.
• Send only U.S. money.
• If a grown-up is helping you, he or she may write a check (unless the directions tell you not to send checks).
• Send all money directly to the suppliers—their addresses are listed with their offers.

Getting Your Stuff

Expect to wait **four to eight weeks** for your stuff to arrive. Sometimes you have to wait longer. Remember, suppliers get thousands of requests each year. Please be patient! If you wait a long time and your offer still doesn't come, you may be using the wrong edition. This is the **1996** edition—the offers in this book will only be good for 1995 and 1996!

Making Sure You Get Your Request

The Free Stuff Editors have tried to make the directions for using this book as clear as possible, to make sure you get what you send for. But you must follow **all** of the directions **exactly** as they're written, or the supplier will not be able to answer your request. If you're confused about the directions, ask a grown-up to help you.

Do's and Don'ts:

- **Do** use a ballpoint pen. Typing and using a computer are okay, too.
- **Do** print. Cursive can be difficult to read.
- **Do** print your name, address, and zip code clearly and fully on the postcard or on the envelope **and** on the letter you send—sometimes envelopes and letters get separated after they reach the supplier. Do not abbreviate anything except state names. Abbreviations can be confusing.
- **Do** send the correct amount of U.S. money, but don't use pennies.
- **Do** tape the coins to the letter you send them with. If you don't tape them, the money might rip the envelope and fall out.
- **Do** use a **9½-inch-long** self-addressed, stamped envelope when the instructions ask for a "long" envelope.

- **Do not** use this **1996** edition **after** 1996.
- **Do not** ask for more than **one** of an item, unless the directions say you can.
- **Do not** stack coins in the envelope.
- **Do not** seal your long self-addressed, stamped envelope. The suppliers need to be able to put the item you ordered in the envelope you send.
- **Do not** ask Meadowbrook Press to send you any of the items listed in the book unless you are ordering the Meadowbrook offers from pages 46 or 53. The publishers of this book do not carry items belonging to other suppliers. They do not supply refunds, either.

Follow all the rules to avoid disappointment!

What to Do If You Aren't Satisfied:

If you have complaints about any offer, or if you don't receive the items you sent for within eight to ten weeks, contact the Free Stuff Editors. Before you complain, please reread the directions. Are you sure you followed them properly? Are you using this **1996** edition **after** 1996? (The offers in this book are only good for 1995 and 1996.) The Free Stuff Editors won't be able to send you the item, but they can make sure that any suppliers who don't fulfill requests are dropped from next year's *Free Stuff for Kids*. For **each** of your complaints you must tell us the name of the offer as it appears in the book, the page number of the offer, and the date you sent your request. Without this information, we may not be able to help you. We'd like to know which offers you like and what kind of new offers you'd like us to add to next year's edition. So don't be bashful—write us a letter. Send your complaints or suggestions to:

The Free Stuff Editors
Meadowbrook Press
18318 Minnetonka Boulevard
Deephaven, MN 55391

Free Stuff for Kids Checklist

Use this checklist each time you send out a request. It will help you follow directions **exactly** and prevent mistakes. Put a check mark in the box each time you complete a task—you can photocopy this page and use it again and again.

For all requests:
- ❏ I sent my request during either **1995** or **1996**.

When sending postcards and letters:
- ❏ I used a ballpoint pen.
- ❏ I printed neatly and carefully.
- ❏ I asked for the correct item (only one).
- ❏ I wrote to the correct supplier.
- ❏ I double-checked the supplier's address.

When sending postcards only:
- ❏ I put my return address on the postcard.
- ❏ I applied a postcard stamp (if the postage wasn't preprinted).

When sending letters only:
- ❏ I put my return address on the letter.
- ❏ I included a **9½-inch** self-addressed, stamped envelope (if the directions asked for one).
- ❏ I included the correct amount of money (if the directions asked for money).
- ❏ I put my return address on the envelope.
- ❏ I applied a **first-class stamp.**

When sending a long self-addressed, stamped envelope:
- ❏ I used a **9½-inch-long** envelope.
- ❏ I put my address on the front of the envelope.
- ❏ I put my return address in the upper left-hand corner of the envelope.
- ❏ I left the envelope unsealed.
- ❏ I applied a **first-class stamp.**

When responding to one-dollar offers:
- ❏ I sent U.S. money.
- ❏ I enclosed a one-dollar bill with my letter instead of coins.

When sending coins:
- ❏ I sent U.S. money.
- ❏ I taped the coins to my letter.
- ❏ I did not stack the coins on top of each other.
- ❏ I did not use pennies. (Extra coins make the envelope heavier and may require extra postage.)

SPORTS

Chicago Bulls

Cheer on the most successful basketball team of the 1990s, the Chicago Bulls, as they stampede toward another NBA title. Their fan pack includes a pocket schedule, bumper sticker, fan letter, and fan club information (depending on availability).

Directions:	Write your request on paper and put it in an envelope. You must enclose a **long self-addressed, stamped envelope.**
Write to:	The Chicago Bulls ATTN: Fan Mail 1901 West Madison Chicago, IL 60612
Ask for:	Chicago Bulls fan pack

The Atlanta Hawks

The Atlanta Hawks are one of the hottest teams in the Eastern Conference of the NBA. Get in on the excitement by sending for their fan pack, which includes a bumper sticker and pocket schedule.

Directions:	Write your request on paper and put it in an envelope. You must enclose a **long self-addressed, stamped envelope.**
Write to:	Atlanta Hawks ATTN: Fan Mail PR Department One CNN Center, Suite 405 Atlanta, GA 30303
Ask for:	Atlanta Hawks bumper sticker

Detroit Pistons

Pistons fans will love this special fan pack offer from their favorite team. It features a team schedule and an 8½-by-11-inch team photo (depending on availability).

Directions:	Write your name, address, and request on a postcard.
Write to:	Detroit Pistons ATTN: Fan Mail Two Championship Drive Auburn Hills, MI 48326
Ask for:	Detroit Pistons fan pack

Washington Bullets

The Bullets feature the exciting combination of former University of Michigan stars Chris Weber and Juwan Howard. Cheer them on to victory with this fan pack, which includes a pocket schedule and bumper sticker (depending on availability).

Directions:	Write your request on paper and put it in an envelope. You must enclose a **long self-addressed, stamped envelope.**
Write to:	Washington Bullets ATTN: Fan Mail USAir Arena Landover, MD 20785
Ask for:	Washington Bullets fan pack

Hall of Fame Pamphlet

Where can you see a pair of bronzed, size-twenty-two sneakers? At the Basketball Hall of Fame! Read all about this "fan-tastic" museum where the history of basketball comes alive.

Directions:	Write your request on paper and put it in an envelope. You must enclose a **long self-addressed, stamped envelope.**
Write to:	Basketball Hall of Fame 1150 West Columbus Avenue Springfield, MA 01105
Ask for:	HOF pamphlet

NFL Team Fan Packs

Support your favorite NFL team by sending away for one of these great NFL fan packs. Each pack features a colorful NFL poster with a letter from your team, team trivia, fun facts, and information on how to join your team's kids club. Choose any NFL team, or a special fan pack covering the whole NFL.

Directions:	Write your name, address, and request on a postcard.
Write to:	ATTN: Free Stuff for Kids Request Cadmus Sports Marketing P.O. Box 93303 Atlanta, GA 30377-0303
Ask for:	NFL team fan pack (*You must specify the team you want.*)

Washington Capitals

"Caps" fans will love this offer from the Washington Capitals. Their fan pack includes team information sheets, schedule, souvenir brochure, and bumper sticker (depending on availability).

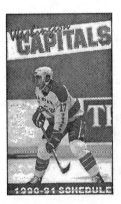

Directions:	Write your request on paper and put it in an envelope. You must enclose a **long self-addressed, stamped envelope.**
Write to:	Washington Capitals ATTN: Fan Mail USAir Arena Landover, MD 20785
Ask for:	Washington Capitals fan pack

Hockey Cards

Keep track of the hottest players in the NHL with your very own set of hockey cards. Start your collection with this set of ten cards, each featuring a player photo on the front and career statistics on the back.

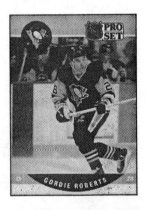

Directions:	Write your request on paper and put it in an envelope. You must enclose a **long self-addressed, stamped envelope** and **50¢.**
Write to:	DANORS Department H 5721 Funston Street, Bay 14 Hollywood, FL 33023
Ask for:	10 hockey cards

HOCKEY

Rochester Americans

The Rochester Americans are one of the most successful minor league hockey teams in the country. Add their hefty fan pack to your collection. It includes a red, white, and blue window decal, logo sticker, bumper sticker, merchandise catalog, and a team picture and magnet schedule (depending on availability).

Directions:	Write your request on paper and put it in an envelope. You must enclose a **long self-addressed, stamped envelope.**
Write to:	The Rochester Americans ATTN: Fan Pack 100 Exchange Street, Room 228 Rochester, NY 14614-2192
Ask for:	Rochester Americans fan pack

Providence Bruins

Check out "What's Bruin" with a fan pack from the Providence Bruins, the minor league hockey affiliate of the Boston Bruins. It features a pocket schedule and a bumper sticker.

Directions:	Write your request on paper and put it in an envelope. You must enclose a **long self-addressed, stamped envelope.**
Write to:	Providence Bruins ATTN: Fan Mail One LaSalle Square Providence, RI 02903
Ask for:	Providence Bruins fan pack

Minnesota Twins

The Minnesota Twins have a can't-miss offer. Send for a schedule, brochure, and photo packet (depending on availability) from the team that features two-time World Series hero Kirby Puckett.

Directions:	Write your request on paper and put it in an envelope. You must enclose a **long self-addressed, stamped envelope.**
Write to:	ATTN: Fan Mail Minnesota Twins 501 Chicago Avenue South Minneapolis, MN 55415
Ask for:	Minnesota Twins pocket schedule, novelty brochure, and team/player photos

New York Yankees

One of the American League's oldest and most celebrated teams has an offer that's a home run. Send for a New York Yankees bumper sticker, schedule, and decal (depending on availability).

Directions:	Write your request on paper and put it in an envelope. You must enclose a **long self-addressed, stamped envelope.**
Write to:	Community Relations Department c/o Yankees Fan Pack New York Yankees Yankees Stadium Bronx, NY 10451
Ask for:	New York Yankees bumper sticker, pocket schedule, and decal

Texas Rangers

The Texas Rangers are a powerhouse in the American League West. Cheer them on with this fan pack, which includes a team schedule, logo sticker, and souvenir list (depending on availability).

Directions:	Write your request on paper and put it in an envelope. You must enclose a **long self-addressed, stamped envelope.**
Write to:	Souvenir Department Texas Rangers P.O. Box 90111 Arlington, TX 76004-3111
Ask for:	Texas Rangers schedule, sticker, and souvenir list

Philadelphia Phillies

Here's a fun offer from the 1993 National League champs, the Philadelphia Phillies. Their fan pack includes a pocket schedule, team logo sticker, and two player photocards (depending on availability). Or, fans of the team's mascot can ask for a "Phillie Phanatic" decal and photocard.

Directions:	Write your request on paper and put it in an envelope. You must enclose a **long self-addressed, stamped envelope.**
Write to:	Phillies Fan Mail P.O. Box 7575 Philadelphia, PA 19101
Ask for:	· Philadelphia Phillies pocket schedule, logo sticker, and two player photo cards **or** · Phillie Phanatic sticker and photocard

Houston Astros

Did you know the Houston Astros were the first team to play under a domed stadium and on artificial turf? Their fan pack features a schedule, logo sticker, and player photo (depending on availability).

Directions:	Write your request on paper and put it in an envelope. You must enclose a **long self-addressed, stamped envelope.**
Write to:	Houston Astros Public Relations P.O. Box 288 Houston, TX 77001-0288
Ask for:	Houston Astros schedule, logo sticker, and player photo

Olympic Baseball

Send away for this fantastic offer for baseball cards. You'll get a set of twenty-five cards from the 1987 USA Baseball Team, featuring such major league stars as Frank Thomas, Jim Abbott, and Ed Sprague. You'll also receive information about USA Baseball, the organization that selects Olympic baseball players.

Directions:	Write your request on paper and put it in an envelope. You must enclose a **long self-addressed, stamped envelope** and **three first-class stamps.**
Write to:	ATTN: 1987 Card Set USA Baseball 2160 Greenwood Avenue Trenton, NJ 08609
Ask for:	1987 card set

Toledo Mud Hens

Beef up your collection with this offer from a world-famous minor league baseball team, the Toledo Mud Hens. It features their mascot, a bat-swinging bird named Muddy the Mud Hen. You'll receive a Mud Hens logo sticker, Muddy baseball cards, a pocket schedule, and a personalized note from Muddy!

Directions:	Write your request on paper and put it in an envelope. You must enclose a **long self-addressed, stamped envelope.**
Write to:	Mud Hens Free Stuff Toledo Mud Hens 2901 Key Street Maumee, OH 43537
Ask for:	Mud Hens logo sticker, Muddy baseball cards, pocket schedule, and note from Muddy

Durham Bulls

Be the first kid on your block to get a fan pack from the Durham Bulls. It features their famous mascot, a smoke-breathing bull named Wool E. Bull. It includes a Bulls' player baseball card, pocket schedule, souvenir list, and a Wool E. Bull card. You can also become a member of the Jr. Bulls Fan Club.

Directions:	Write your request on paper and put it in an envelope. You must enclose a **long self-addressed, stamped envelope.**
Write to:	Durham Bulls Public Relations Department P.O. Box 507 Durham, NC 27702
Ask for:	Durham Bulls player card, Wool E. Bull card, pocket schedule, and souvenir list

Hickory Crawdads

The Hickory Crawdads' mascot, Conrad the Crawdad, is the only crayfish in the world who knows how to play baseball! You can become a member of his fan club. Send for the Crawdads' fan pack and you'll receive a membership certificate, team sticker, schedule, and souvenir brochure.

Directions:	Write your request on paper and put it in an envelope. You must enclose a **9-by-12-inch self-addressed, stamped envelope.**
Write to:	Conrad's Pen Pal Club Hickory Crawdads P.O. Box 1268 Hickory, NC 28603
Ask for:	Hickory Crawdads pocket schedule, souvenir brochure, team stickers, and certificate

Fort Wayne Wizards

You won't believe your eyes when you see the Fort Wayne Wizards' fan pack. It features a sticker of their mascot, Wayne the Wizard, holding a baseball that's also a crystal ball. You'll also receive a pocket schedule, souvenir list, and a baseball card of Wayne.

Directions:	Write your name, address, and request on paper and put it in an envelope.
Write to:	Fort Wayne Wizards Memorial Stadium c/o Wizards Fan Pack 4000 Parnell Avenue Fort Wayne, IN 46805-1498
Ask for:	Fort Wayne Wizards pocket schedule, bumper sticker, souvenir list, and baseball card of Wayne the Wizard

Phoenix Firebirds

Become a fan of the Phoenix Firebirds baseball team and get your own copy of what's easily the hottest sticker in minor league baseball. The Firebirds' fan pack includes a logo sticker, schedule, catalog, and information on the Firebirds Li'l Birds Club.

Directions:	Write your request on paper and put it in an envelope. You must enclose a **long self-addressed, stamped envelope.**
Write to:	Firebirds Fan Pack Phoenix Firebirds Baseball P.O. Box 8528 Scottsdale, AZ 85252-8528
Ask for:	Phoenix Firebirds pocket schedule, team catalog, logo sticker, and information on the Li'l Birds Club

Prince William Cannons

The Prince William Cannons are a minor league baseball team with a major offer for you. Get ready to blast off with their powerful logo, which features a baseball shooting out of a cannon. Their fan pack includes a bumper sticker, schedule, and souvenir list.

Directions:	Write your request on paper and put it in an envelope. You must enclose a **long self-addressed, stamped envelope.**
Write to:	Prince William Cannons c/o Cannons Fun Pack P.O. Box 2148 Woodbridge, VA 22193
Ask for:	Prince William Cannons bumper sticker, schedule, and souvenir list

Lake Elsinore Storm

The Lake Elsinore Storm, from California, are one of the hottest new minor league baseball teams. Add their electrifying logo to your collection. You'll receive a pocket schedule, logo sticker, and souvenir list.

Directions:	Write your request on paper and put it in an envelope. You must enclose a **long self-addressed, stamped envelope.**
Write to:	Free Stuff Lake Elsinore Storm P.O. Box 535 Lake Elsinore, CA 92531
Ask for:	Lake Elsinore Storm schedule, sticker, and souvenir list

Portland Sea Dogs

Send away for a truly unique offer from the Portland Sea Dogs, whose logo features a seal with a baseball bat in its mouth! Send for their fan pack and you'll receive a tattoo of their logo, a brochure, pocket schedule, and button (depending on availability).

Directions:	Write your request on paper and put it in an envelope. You must enclose a **9-by-12-inch self-addressed, stamped envelope** with **two first-class stamps**.
Write to:	Fan Mail/Souvenir Store Portland Sea Dogs P.O. Box 636 Portland, ME 04104
Ask for:	Portland Sea Dogs brochure, pocket schedule, tattoo, and button

The Quakes

Become a fan of the team with the wackiest name in the minor leagues, the Rancho Cucamonga Quakes. The 1994 California League Champions, the Quakes offer an exciting logo sticker, schedule, and souvenir brochure.

Directions:	Write your request on paper and put it in an envelope. You must enclose a **long self-addressed, stamped envelope**.
Write to:	Quakes Fan Pack P.O. Box 4139 Rancho Cucamonga, CA 91729
Ask for:	Quakes schedule, sticker, and souvenir brochure

MINOR LEAGUE BASEBALL

The Warthogs

Here's a great offer from the Winston-Salem Warthogs, a team with a crazy mascot! Get hold of this fantastic logo by sending away for their fan pack, which includes a sticker, schedule, and souvenir list.

Directions:	Write your request on paper and put it in an envelope. You must enclose a **long self-addressed, stamped envelope.**
Write to:	Winston-Salem Warthogs P.O. Box 4488 Winston-Salem, NC 27115
Ask for:	Winston-Salem Warthogs sticker, schedule, and souvenir list

Buffalo Bisons

Here's a great offer from the Buffalo, New York, minor league baseball team, the Bisons. Their zany logo features team mascot Buster T. Bison. Send for their fan pack and you'll get a sticker, player cards, schedule, and souvenir list.

Directions:	Write your request on paper and put it in an envelope. You must enclose a **9-by-12-inch self-addressed envelope.** *No postage required.*
Write to:	FREE BISONS STUFF P.O. Box 450 Buffalo, NY 14205
Ask for:	Buffalo Bisons fan pack

24

Luge

Did you know "luge" is the French word for sled? This exciting winter sport has been part of the Olympics since 1964. You can learn more about sliders and their sleds by sending for this pamphlet.

Directions:	Write your request on paper and put it in an envelope. You must enclose a **long self-addressed, stamped envelope.**
Write to:	U.S. Luge Association P.O. Box 651 Lake Placid, NY 12946
Ask for:	Luge pamphlet

Bobsled

Find out about the exciting Winter Olympic sport of bobsledding and what it takes to make the U.S. Bobsled Team. Send for this great offer from the U.S. Bobsled & Skeleton Federation, which includes a decal and informational brochure.

SUPPORTING

UNITED STATES
BOBSLED & SKELETON
FEDERATION

Directions:	Write your request on paper and put it in an envelope. You must enclose a **long self-addressed, stamped envelope.**
Write to:	U.S. Bobsled & Skeleton Federation P.O. Box 828 Lake Placid, NY 12946
Ask for:	U.S. Bobsled & Skeleton Federation sticker and informational brochure

Curling

Learn all about curling, one of the newest official Winter Olympic sports. Curling is played on ice with huge, heavy curling "stones." The U.S. Curling Associations offer features the curling rules of play, and an informational brochure covering the history of this sport.

Directions:	Write your request on paper and put it in an envelope. You must enclose a **long self-addressed, stamped envelope** with **two first-class stamps.**
Write to:	U.S. Curling Association P.O. Box 866 Stevens Point, WI 54481-0866
Ask for:	Curling Rules of Play and Fitness/Finesse brochure

Badminton

Badminton is one of the world's quickest and most popular sports. On a smash, a shuttlecock can reach speeds up to 200 miles per hour! Show your support for the world's fastest racquet sport by sending for this sticker featuring Izzy, the official Atlanta 1996 Olympic mascot.

Directions:	Write your request on paper and put it in an envelope. You must enclose a **long self-addressed, stamped envelope** and **50¢.**
Write to:	United States Badminton Association One Olympic Plaza Colorado Springs, CO 80909
Ask for:	Izzy badminton sticker

MEADOWBROOK PRESS

1996
EDITION

U.S.
MAIL

STICKERS

Love in the Jungle

Recreate a love scene from Disney's hit movie *The Lion King* with this sheet of cute stickers. You'll receive nine stickers featuring Mufasa and Sarabi that you can arrange to make your own scenes.

Directions:	Write your request on paper and put it in an envelope. You must enclose **$1.00**.
Write to:	Mr. Rainbows Department LK10 P.O. Box 908 Rio Grande, NJ 08242
Ask for:	Love in the Jungle stickers

Fuzzy or Shiny Stickers

Here are more of your favorite *Lion King* characters including Simba, Timon, Nala, and Pumba. Send for two sheets of five stickers. You can choose either fuzzy or shiny.

Directions:	Write your request on paper and put it in an envelope. You must enclose **$1.00** for **each** sheet you request.
Write to:	Mr. Rainbows Department LK20 P.O. Box 908 Rio Grande, NJ 08242
Ask for:	• Lion King fuzzy stickers **or** • Lion King shiny stickers

Coca-Cola Stickers

"Trink Coca-Cola" is German for "Drink Coca-Cola." This sticker-postcard features the Coke trademark in six different languages, including German, Russian, and Chinese.

Directions:	Write your name, address, and request on a postcard.
Write to:	The Coca-Cola Company Consumer Information Center Department FS P.O. Drawer 1734 Atlanta, GA 30301
Ask for:	Coca-Cola sticker-postcard *(Limit 1 per request.)*

Scratch-and-Smell

Here's a flavorful offer for free scratch-and-smell stickers. Just scratch the stickers on the sheet and you'll smell four different flavors: cherry, orange sherbet, banana pudding, and grape juice.

Directions:	Write your request on paper and put it in an envelope. You must enclose a **long self-addressed, stamped envelope.**
Write to:	Mr. Rainbows Department FS10 P.O. Box 908 Rio Grande, NJ 08242
Ask for:	Scratch-and-smell stickers

Dinosaur Action Stickers

Catch your favorite fearsome dinosaurs in action with this colorful offer. You'll receive stickers of eight different dinosaurs, including Tyrannosaurus Rex, Triceratops, and Pterodactyl.

Directions:	Write your request on paper and put it in an envelope. You must enclose **50¢.**
Write to:	Mr. Rainbows Department FS13 P.O. Box 908 Rio Grande, NJ 08242
Ask for:	Dinosaur action stickers

Dinosaur Sticker Scene

Use your imagination to create your own prehistoric scenes. This fun offer features a sheet of twelve different dinosaurs, plus a land scene to stick them on.

Directions:	Write your request on paper and put it in an envelope. You must enclose a **long self-addressed, stamped envelope** and **25¢.**
Write to:	Phyllis Goodstein Department DS P.O. Box 912 Levittown, NY 11756-0912
Ask for:	Dinosaur stickers

Prismatic Animals

This great set of sparkling prismatic stickers will brighten up your class notebooks and papers. It features twelve different stickers of adorable animals, including bunnies, chicks, and skunks.

Zoo Stickers

Do you like going to the zoo? This great packet of stickers features eleven of your favorite animals. Give them to your friends, stick them on your letters, or create your very own animal collection.

Directions:	Write your request on paper and put it in an envelope. You must enclose a **long self-addressed, stamped envelope** and **$1.00.**
Write to:	Stickers 'N' Stuff, Inc. Department CLA P.O. Box 430 Louisville, CO 80027
Ask for:	Prismatic animal stickers

Directions:	Write your request on paper and put it in an envelope. You must enclose a **long self-addressed, stamped envelope** and **25¢.**
Write to:	SAV-ON Department ZS P.O. Box 1356 Gwinn, MI 49841
Ask for:	Zoo stickers

Flintstones

These funny stickers feature your favorite Flintstones characters in action. You'll laugh at Fred, Dino, and Barney as they play baseball, surf, and fish.

Directions:	Write your request on paper and put it in an envelope. You must enclose **$1.00.**
Write to:	Mr. Rainbows Department FS P.O. Box 908 Rio Grande, NJ 08242
Ask for:	Flintstone stickers

Santa Stickers

Get hold of these great stickers of Old Saint Nick that will remind you and your friends to say "ho, ho, ho" all through the year. You'll receive a colorful sheet of six stickers with Santa in various poses.

Directions:	Write your request on paper and put it in an envelope. You must enclose **$1.00.**
Write to:	Joan Nykorchuk 13236 North Seventh Street, #4 Suite 237 Phoenix, AZ 85022
Ask for:	Santa Claus stickers

Glowing Stickers

By day, they look like ordinary stickers; by night, they glow! These glow-in-the-dark stickers will add a friendly shine to your collection. You'll get one sheet with footprints and one sheet with animal faces.

Sports Stickers

Are you a sports fan? If you are, you'll really **score** with these baseball, football, basketball, and **soccer** stickers. You'll receive one sheet filled with **fifteen** iridescent stickers of a random sport.

Directions:	Write your request on paper and put it in an envelope. You must enclose **$1.00.**
Write to:	Mr. Rainbows Department PC6 P.O. Box 908 Rio Grande, NJ 08242
Ask for:	Glow-in-the-dark footprints and animal faces

Directions:	Write your request on paper and put it in an envelope. You must enclose a **long self-addressed, stamped envelope** and **25¢.**
Write to:	Phyllis Goodstein Department SS P.O. Box 912 Levittown, NY 11756-0912
Ask for:	Sports stickers

Sweetheart Stickers

Do you have a special sweetheart? Brighten up his or her day with these cute valentine stickers. You'll get over seventy-five stickers with phrases like "Be Mine," "I'm Yours," and "You're Cute."

Directions:	Write your request on paper and put it in an envelope. You must enclose a **long self-addressed, stamped envelope** and **50¢.**
Write to:	Surprise Gift of the Month Club Department SWST P.O. Box 1 Stony Point, NY 10980
Ask for:	Sweetheart stickers

Lots of Stickers

These small, round stickers are colorful, cute, and a great way to highlight a letter to your pen pal or other friends. You'll get a sheet of one hundred stickers. You can choose a sheet of star, party-time, or rainbows-and-butterflies stickers.

Directions:	Write your request on paper and put it in an envelope. You must enclose **$1.00** for **each** sheet you request.
Write to:	The Very Best Sticker Company Department MPA P.O. Box 2838 Long Beach, CA 90801-2838
Ask for:	• 100 rainbows-and-butterflies stickers **or** • 100 star stickers **or** • 100 party-time stickers

Personalized Decals

Now you can label lockers, books, folders, and other important stuff by sending for these handy personalized decals. Choose up to ten letters and numbers to make up your name, phone number, or anything else!

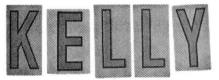

Directions:	Write your request on paper and put it in an envelope. You must enclose a **long self-addressed, stamped envelope** and **$1.00.**
Write to:	Parker Flags and Pennants 5750 Plunkett Street Suite 5 Hollywood, FL 33023
Ask for:	Personalized letter decals *(You must specify up to 10 letters or numbers for your request.)*

Slang Stickers

Get up to speed by sending for these fast-paced, wacky slang stickers. You'll receive nine stickers featuring phrases like "Gotta Go!" "Enuff for Now," and "C-Ya!"

Directions:	Write your request on paper and put it in an envelope. You must enclose a **long self-addressed, stamped envelope** and **50¢.**
Write to:	Surprise Gift of the Month Club Department WSST P.O. Box 1 Stony Point, NY 10980
Ask for:	Wacky slang stickers

Puffy Rainbow Stickers

These wonderful rainbow stickers will brighten up your day with lots of color. Their soft, puffy surface adds a fun dimension to your class notebooks and folders. You'll receive two rainbow stickers.

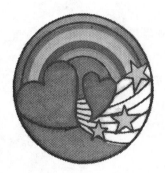

Directions:	Write your request on paper and put it in an envelope. You must enclose a **long self-addressed, stamped envelope** and **25¢.**
Write to:	SAV-ON Department PRS P.O. Box 1356 Gwinn, MI 49841
Ask for:	Puffy rainbow stickers

Sticker Dolls

Get hold of one of these unique, reusable sticker dolls. You'll receive a booklet with over a dozen stickers. You can use the stickers over and over again to "dress up" your sticker doll. Choose "Little Lisa" doll, "Baby Bear" doll, or "Dinosaur" doll.

Directions:	Write your request on paper and put it in an envelope. You must enclose **$1.00.**
Write to:	Eleanor Curran Department PD 530 Leonard Street Brooklyn, NY 11222
Ask for:	• Little Lisa sticker doll **or** • Baby Bear sticker doll **or** • Dinosaur sticker doll

SCHOOL SUPPLIES

Presidents Ruler

Now you can learn math and history at the same time. This foot-long ruler marks both inches and centimeters and features pictures of every president from Washington to Clinton. On the back, you'll find pictures of U.S. flags and the lyrics to "The Star-Spangled Banner."

Directions:	Write your request on paper and put it in an envelope. You must enclose **$1.00.**
Write to:	Smiles 'N' Things Department PFR P.O. Box 974 Claremont, CA 91711-0974
Ask for:	Presidential ruler

Action Scene Ruler

You have to see this ruler to believe it! With every turn of the wrist, you'll watch a space scene change before your eyes. The foot-long ruler marks both inches and centimeters and lists a handy multiplication table on the back.

Directions:	Write your request on paper and put it in an envelope. You must enclose **90¢.**
Write to:	Safe Child P.O. Box 40-1594 Brooklyn, NY 11240-1594
Ask for:	Action scene ruler

Bracelet Pen

Do you lose pens and pencils all the time? Here's a pen you'll never lose. When you're finished writing, it wraps around your wrist and becomes a handy bracelet!

Directions:	Write your request on paper and put it in an envelope. You must enclose a **long self-addressed, stamped envelope** and **$1.00**.
Write to:	Neetstuf Department N3 P.O. Box 353 Rio Grande, NJ 08242
Ask for:	Bracelet pen

Friendship Pen

You've heard of friendship bracelets. Now you can get a friendship pen. You'll receive a **complete** friendship pen kit, including a pen, embroidery thread, and instructions. Give your best buddy a personalized present!

Directions:	Write your request on paper and put it in an envelope. You must enclose **75¢.**
Write to:	Surprise Gift of the Month Club Department FP P.O. Box 1 Stony Point, NY 10980
Ask for:	Friendship pen

Assorted Pencil Tops

Decorate all your pens and pencils with these cute and zany pencil tops. You'll receive five assorted designs, including a pumpkin head, potato head, and other figures.

Directions:	Write your request on paper and put it in an envelope. You must enclose **$1.00**.
Write to:	Lightning Enterprises P.O. Box 16121 West Palm Beach, FL 33416
Ask for:	Assorted pencil tops

Woodpecker Tops

Here's a great way to avoid the homework blues. These cute little woodpeckers fit on the ends of your pen or pencil and bob happily up and down as you write. You'll receive four pencil tops.

Directions:	Write your request on paper and put it in an envelope. You must enclose **$1.00**.
Write to:	Eleanor Curran Department W 530 Leonard Street Brooklyn, NY 11222
Ask for:	Woodpecker pencil tops

Shark or Gator Pencil

This big, bright-orange pencil will be one of your favorites. It comes with your choice of a rubber shark or alligator biting on the end of it.

Directions:	Write your request on paper and put it in an envelope. You must enclose a **long self-addressed, stamped envelope** and **50¢**.
Write to:	DANORS Department P 5721 Funston Street Hollywood, FL 33023
Ask for:	• Shark pencil **or** • Alligator pencil

Enormous Erasers

Clean up your mistakes for the entire school year with these giant erasers. You can choose from a lazy-looking alligator or two big oranges.

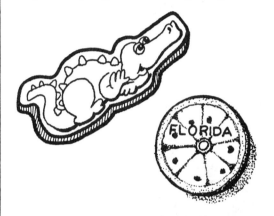

Directions:	Write your request on paper and put it in an envelope. You must enclose a **long self-addressed, stamped envelope** and **50¢**.
Write to:	DANORS Department FS 5721 Funston Street, Bay 14 Hollywood, FL 33023
Ask for:	• Alligator eraser **or** • 2 orange erasers

Assorted Erasers

Make an instant eraser collection with this fun and colorful assortment. You'll receive fifteen miniature erasers featuring all sorts of objects, including ice cream cones, Easter eggs, rabbits, kittens, and puppies.

Dinosaur Erasers

The ferocious dinosaurs pictured on these erasers are ready to eat up all your mistakes! You'll receive two erasers, one featuring Tyrannosaurus Rex and the other featuring Stegosaurus.

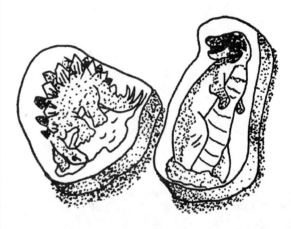

Directions:	Write your request on paper and put it in an envelope. You must enclose **$1.00.**
Write to:	Lightning Enterprises P.O. Box 16121 West Palm Beach, FL 33416
Ask for:	Assorted mini-erasers

Directions:	Write your request on paper and put it in an envelope. You must enclose **70¢.**
Write to:	Safe Child P.O. Box 40-1594 Brooklyn, NY 11240-1594
Ask for:	Dinosaur erasers

Personalized Stationery

Add an extra personal touch to the letters you write to friends with this personalized stationery. You'll receive four sheets of paper with your own name at the top.

Directions:	Write your request on paper and put it in an envelope. You must enclose a **9-by-12-inch self-addressed, stamped envelope** and **25¢**.
Write to:	Houser's Unlimited Department L 43826 Birchtree Avenue Lancaster, CA 93534-5011
Ask for:	Personalized stationery *(You must specify the name you want to appear on the stationery.)*

Paper and Envelopes

Stock up on your letter-writing materials with these colorful supplies in assorted designs. You can get a set of twenty pieces of writing paper with fifteen envelopes or a set of fifty assorted envelopes in great colors and designs. You must specify which set you want.

Directions:	Write your request on paper and put it in an envelope. You must enclose **$1.00** for **each** set you request.
Write to:	Surprise Gift of the Month Club Department ST/EV P.O. Box 1 Stony Point, NY 10980
Ask for:	• 20 letters and 15 envelopes **or** • 50 assorted envelopes

Kids' Scissors

These scissors will work great for all your school projects. They cut paper perfectly, and feature a cute design on the front. Best of all, their rounded points mean you can carry them safely.

Directions:	Write your request on paper and put it in an envelope. You must enclose **75¢**.
Write to:	Surprise Gift of the Month Club Department KS P.O. Box 1 Stony Point, NY 10980
Ask for:	Kids' scissors

Football Key Chain

Keep track of your valuable house keys and locker keys with this fun, football key chain. This puffy, squeezable key chain is so big you should never lose your keys.

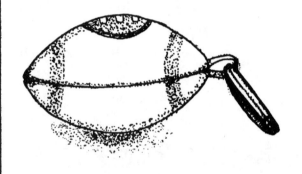

Directions:	Write your request on paper and put it in an envelope. You must enclose **$1.00**.
Write to:	Safe Child P.O. Box 40-1594 Brooklyn, NY 11240-1594
Ask for:	Football key chain

READING

BOOKMARKS

New Moon Bookmark

New Moon: The Magazine for Girls and Their Dreams is an advertising-free international magazine with stories by and about girls all over the world. This offer features a nifty bookmark and a pamphlet with more information about this terrific magazine.

Directions:	Write your request on paper and put it in an envelope. You must enclose a **long self-addressed, stamped envelope.**
Write to:	New Moon P.O. Box 3620 Duluth, MN 55803 ATTN: Bookmark Offer
Ask for:	New Moon bookmark and pamphlet

Funny Poetry

A Bad Case of the Giggles is an illustrated book full of hilarious poems chosen by kids your age. The bookmark you'll get features a few of the funniest poems from the *Giggles* book.

Directions:	Write your request on paper and put it in an envelope. You must enclose a **long self-addressed, stamped envelope.**
Write to:	Meadowbrook Press Department BCG 18318 Minnetonka Boulevard Deephaven, MN 55391
Ask for:	A Bad Case of the Giggles bookmark

Personalized Bookmark

Reading is more fun with a personalized bookmark keeping your place as you read through your favorite books. This colorful bookmark is laminated and comes with your first name on it.

Directions:	Write your request on paper and put it in an envelope. You must enclose a **long self-addressed, stamped envelope** and **25¢.**
Write to:	Houser's Unlimited Department B 43826 Birchtree Avenue Lancaster, CA 93534-5011
Ask for:	Personalized bookmark *(You must specify the name you want to appear on the bookmark.)*

"LUV" Bookmark

Learn how to do needlepoint and create your very own bookmark at the same time. You'll receive a complete needlepoint kit, including thread, a bookmark, and instructions on how to stitch the word "LUV" on it.

Directions:	Write your request on paper and put it in an envelope. You must enclose a **long self-addressed, stamped envelope** and **$1.00.**
Write to:	Surprise Gift of the Month Club Department NB P.O. Box 1 Stony Point, NY 10980
Ask for:	Needlepoint bookmark

Cartoon Bookmark

Now some of your favorite cartoon characters can join you as you read. The bookmark you'll get will feature one of such characters as the Bernstein Bears, Bambi, and Wile E. Coyote.

Directions:	Write your request on paper and put it in an envelope. You must enclose a **long self-addressed, stamped envelope** and **25¢.**
Write to:	SAV-ON Department CCB P.O. Box 1356 Gwinn, MI 49841
Ask for:	Cartoon characters bookmark

Felt Bookmark

Here's a colorful bookmark celebrating the state of Florida. It's made out of a soft, thick felt material and features a slot in the back to grip the page you want to mark in your book.

Directions:	Write your request on paper and put it in an envelope. You must enclose a **long self-addressed, stamped envelope** and **50¢.**
Write to:	Parker Flags and Pennants 5750 Plunkett Street Suite 5 Hollywood, FL 33023
Ask for:	Souvenir Florida bookmark

Disney Book Cover

Decorate your favorite book by sending away for this sturdy, water-resistant book cover. The colorful design features the all-time favorite Disney character, Mickey Mouse.

Directions:	Write your request on paper and put it in an envelope. You must enclose a **long self-addressed, stamped envelope** and **$1.00.**
Write to:	Creative Fun Razers Department FS P.O. Box 283 Concord, NC 28026
Ask for:	Disney book cover

Dinosaur and Rainbow Book Covers

You'll have the hottest books in town when you get hold of these cool covers. You'll receive two covers: one with an exciting dinosaur scene, and another with a big, colorful rainbow.

Directions:	Write your request on paper and put it in an envelope. You must enclose **$1.00.**
Write to:	Neetstuf Department FS-20 P.O. Box 353 Rio Grande, NJ 08242
Ask for:	Dinosaur and rainbow book covers

Tough Times Reading List

This pamphlet from the American Library Association lists fifty books that can help you understand and live through troubled times. "Life Can Be Tough" describes books for different ages that deal with death, divorce, family separation, and other difficulties.

Directions:	Write your request on paper and put it in an envelope. You must enclose a **long self-addressed, stamped envelope.**
Write to:	American Library Association Graphics Department LCBT 50 East Huron Street Chicago, IL 60611
Ask for:	Life Can Be Tough pamphlet

Friendship Reading List

People who are very different sometimes form the best friendships. "You and Me Together" is a list of books about the deep bonds between people of different ages, including many stories about grandparents and grandchildren.

Directions:	Write your request on paper and put it in an envelope. You must enclose a **long self-addressed, stamped envelope.**
Write to:	American Library Association Graphics Department YMT 50 East Huron Street Chicago, IL 60611
Ask for:	Many Faces, Many Stories pamphlet

Award Winners List

Each year the Coretta Scott King Award goes to African-American authors and illustrators whose children's books promote a better understanding of black culture. Learn about these books by sending for this pamphlet, which lists the award winners and their titles.

Directions:	Write your request on paper and put it in an envelope. You must enclose a **long self-addressed, stamped envelope.**
Write to:	American Library Association Graphics Department CSK 50 East Huron Street Chicago, IL 60611
Ask for:	Coretta Scott King pamphlet

Kids of Color List

Children of color living in the U.S. today experience many ups and downs, joys and tears. Here's a list of great books about "Today's Children of Color" as they go through their first loves, grow up with brothers and sisters, and have fun being kids.

Directions:	Write your request on paper and put it in an envelope. You must enclose a **long self-addressed, stamped envelope.**
Write to:	American Library Association Graphics Department TCOC 50 East Huron Street Chicago, IL 60611
Ask for:	Today's Children of Color pamphlet

Financial Comics

Have you ever wondered how money was invented? These five comic books are easy to read and help you understand interesting things about economics, including what banks do and how the United States trades with other countries. You must specify which comic books you want.

Directions:	Write your name, address, and request on a postcard.
Write to:	Federal Reserve Bank of New York Public Information Department 33 Liberty Street, 13th Floor New York, NY 10045
Ask for:	• Story of Money comic book **or** • Story of Banks comic book **or** • Once Upon a Dime comic book **or** • A Penny Saved . . . comic book **or** • Story of Foreign Trade comic book

Science Fiction Comic

"A Tail from Outer Space" is a wacky science fiction story about a faraway planet ruled by benevolent creatures called "giplings." The creatures have humans as pets! This story drives home the point that we should treat animals on this planet with care and respect.

Directions:	Write your request on paper and put it in an envelope. You must enclose a **long self-addressed, stamped envelope** with **two first-class stamps.**
Write to:	The Fund for Animals 808 Alamo Drive Suite 306 Vacaville, CA 95688
Ask for:	A Tail from Outer Space comic book

Biblical Stories

These colorful, six-panel cards turn three of the most famous stories from the Bible into neat packages of fun. The cards fold out to tell the stories in easy, simple language. Beautiful illustrations accompany the stories. You can choose from the story of Noah, Jonah and the Whale, or David and Goliath.

Directions:	Write your request on paper and put it in an envelope. You must enclose a **long self-addressed, stamped envelope** and **$1.00** for **each** story you request.
Write to:	More Than A Card 4334 Earhart Boulevard New Orleans, LA 70125
Ask for:	• Jonah story-card **or** • Noah story-card **or** • David and Goliath story-card

Girls to the Rescue

Most female characters in fairy tales wait around for Prince Charming to sweep them off their feet. *Girls to the Rescue* is a brand new collection of stories featuring clever, courageous girls who are their own heroes. Send for this bookmark, which features the book's cover and summaries of the stories.

Directions:	Write your request on paper and put it in an envelope. You must enclose a **long self-addressed, stamped envelope.**
Write to:	Meadowbrook Press Department GTR 18318 Minnetonka Boulevard Deephaven, MN 55391
Ask for:	Girls to the Rescue bookmark

Picture Book Poster

Spice up the decorations in your bedroom with a colorful illustration from a children's picture book. You'll receive either this *Old MacDonald Had a Farm* poster, or a poster from a different children's book.

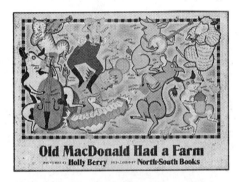

Directions:	Write your request on paper and put it in an envelope. You must enclose a **9-by-12-inch self-addressed envelope** and **three first-class stamps.**
Write to:	North-South Books Free Stuff Poster Offer 1123 Broadway, Suite 800 New York, NY 10010
Ask for:	Free poster

Dr. Suess Postcards

Are you a Dr. Suess fan? Here's a chance to collect five postcards of the famous children's author to send to friends or relatives. The postcards feature Dr. Suess surrounded by some of his best-known cartoon characters, including the Cat in the Hat.

Directions:	Write your request on paper and put it in an envelope. You must enclose a **long self-addressed, stamped envelope.**
Write to:	The Lerner Group Dr. Suess Offer 241 First Avenue North Minneapolis, MN 55401
Ask for:	5 Dr. Suess postcards

MEADOWBROOK PRESS
1996
EDITION

U.S.
MAIL

SCIENCE

SCIENCE PROJECTS

Science Experiments

Thanks to the *Newton's Apple* show on public television, you can try out some fascinating science experiments! With this "Science Try-Its™" sheet, you'll receive all the information you need to perform the experiments at home.

Directions:	Write your request on paper and put it in an envelope. You must enclose a **long self-addressed, stamped envelope.**
Write to:	Newton's Apple Science Try-Its™ c/o Twin Cities Public Television 172 East Fourth Street Saint Paul, MN 55101
Ask for:	Science Try-Its™

Animal Projects

Learn about some animals that live in your neighborhood by sending for this sheet from the American Society for the Prevention of Cruelty to Animals (ASPCA). It describes humane animal projects you can perform—fun and fascinating ways to study animals without disturbing their activities.

Directions:	Write your request on paper and put it in an envelope. You must enclose a **long self-addressed, stamped envelope.**
Write to:	ASPCA Education Department 424 East 92nd Street New York, NY 10128
Ask for:	Humane science projects sheet

Solar Hot Dog Cooker

Learn how to cook a hot dog without using a stove or microwave! These instructions tell you how to build a solar-powered hot dog cooker from cardboard and aluminum foil. It's fascinating and fun for anyone who's into solar energy.

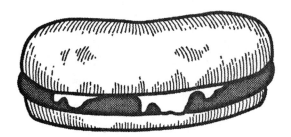

Directions:	Write your request on paper and put it in an envelope. You must enclose a **long self-addressed, stamped envelope** and **50¢.**
Write to:	Energy and Marine Center Department FS-96 P.O. Box 190 Port Richey, FL 34673
Ask for:	Solar hot dog cooker instructions

Bird Feeder

Make your very own bird feeder and observe the birds in your neighborhood with this fun science project. You'll receive complete instructions and materials to make a bird feeder from bread and peanut butter.

Directions:	Write your request on paper and put it in an envelope. You must enclose a **long self-addressed, stamped envelope** and **50¢.**
Write to:	Primarily Kids Incorporated ATTN: Science Series 11075 197th Avenue NW Elk River, MN 55330-2213
Ask for:	Bird feeder instructions

Solar System Facts

This handy chart will put a bunch of fun facts about our solar system right at your fingertips. Find out how long a year lasts on Pluto, how hot it gets on Venus, and what the atmosphere is like on Mars.

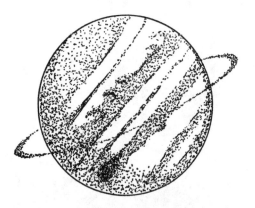

Directions:	Write your request on paper and put it in an envelope. You must enclose a **long self-addressed, stamped envelope** and **25¢.**
Write to:	Solar System Education Department Hansen Planetarium 15 South State Street Salt Lake City, UT 84111-1590
Ask for:	Solar system fact sheet

Planet Stencils

Design your class notebooks and folders with **cool** stencils that are out of this world! You'll receive four tracing figures, including a sun shape, planet Earth, and two others.

Directions:	Write your request on paper and put it in an envelope. You must enclose a **long self-addressed, stamped envelope** and **50¢.**
Write to:	Fax Marketing 460F Carrollton Drive Frederick, MD 21701-6357
Ask for:	Our Earth tracing figures

Astronomy Booklet

The night sky is the best free entertainment in the world. This booklet is the first step to enjoying the show. "Welcome to Amateur Astronomy" describes how to find moons, planets, stars, constellations, clusters, and nebulae with both binoculars and telescopes.

Directions:	Write your name, address, and request on a postcard.
Write to:	Kalmbach Publishing 21027 Crossroads Circle P.O. Box 1612 Waukesha, WI 53187
Ask for:	Welcome to Amateur Astronomy booklet

Seed Packets

Here's your chance to start a window garden and find out if you have a green thumb! You'll receive a packet of vegetable or flower seeds, with instructions on how to grow them.

Directions:	Write your request on paper and put it in an envelope. You must enclose a **long self-addressed, stamped envelope.** *Additional packets are available for **25¢ each.***
Write to:	ACE Hardware Department MP-3 P.O. Box 630 Gwinn, MI 49841
Ask for:	• Packet of flower seeds *or* • Packet of vegetable seeds

Trilobite Fossil Replica

Trilobites were the first creatures on earth to have a pair of eyes and a brain. They were the great-great-grandparents of the modern-day roly-poly bugs. Send for this replica of a prehistoric Trilobite, molded from a genuine Trilobite fossil. You'll also receive information on the history of this interesting creature.

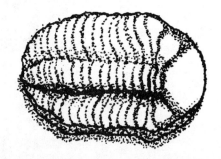

Directions:	Write your request on paper and put it in an envelope. You must enclose a **long self-addressed, stamped envelope** with **two first-class stamps.**
Write to:	Etgen's Science Stuff Free Stuff Trilobite Offer 3600 Whitney Avenue Sacramento, CA 95821
Ask for:	Trilobite fossil replica

Story of Cotton Booklet

Did you know that the ancient Egyptians made and wore cotton clothing? Learn how important the cotton plant has been throughout history. This booklet also describes where the plant is grown today and how it is made into the clothes you wear every day.

Directions:	Write your name, address, and request on a postcard.
Write to:	National Cotton Council Communication Services 1918 North Parkway Memphis, TN 38112
Ask for:	The Story of Cotton booklet

Rain Forests Pamphlet

Tropical rain forests are an extremely important part of the earth's environment. This pamphlet describes what rain forests are, why they are important scientifically, and why they are being destroyed so quickly. You'll also learn about what you can do to help save them.

Directions:	Write your request on paper and put it in an envelope. You must enclose a **long self-addressed, stamped envelope.**
Write to:	Education Department Cincinnati Zoo P.O. Box 198073 Cincinnati, OH 45219-8073
Ask for:	Rain Forests pamphlet

Biomedical Research

Humane and responsible animal research has provided important scientific information leading to cures for human and animal diseases such as polio and rabies. Did you know that the animals used in science labs are very well cared for? Find out about the history and practices of biomedical research. You'll receive a button, newsletter, and colorful booklet.

Directions:	Write your name, address, and request on a postcard.
Write to:	ATTN: FSFK Orders Foundation for Biomedical Research 818 Connecticut Avenue NW Suite 303 Washington, DC 20006
Ask for:	Information on biomedical research and button

WORLD CULTURES

Ceremonial Money

Have you ever seen a bill for a billion dollars? Send for this packet of beautifully made "Hell Bank" notes. In ancient China, special money like this was made for burning at funerals. You'll also receive information on the history of this ceremonial money.

Directions:	Write your request on paper and put it in an envelope. You must enclose a **long self-addressed, stamped envelope.**
Write to:	$1,000,000,000 Bank Note Offer 3600 Whitney Avenue San Francisco, CA 95821
Ask for:	Bank note packet

Rain Sticks

A rain stick is a traditional percussion instrument made by the people of the Brazilian rain forest. Tip one over, and you hear the magical sound of rain falling on leaves. Send for these instructions on how to make your very own rain stick from recycled materials at home. You'll also receive a rain stick bookmark.

Directions:	Write your request on paper and put it in an envelope. You must enclose a **long self-addressed, stamped envelope** and **$1.00.**
Write to:	Tropical Rain Eco-Sticks P.O. Box 32234 San Jose, CA 95152
Ask for:	Tropical Rain Eco-Stick instructions

Amnesty International

Get involved with the work of Amnesty International and help set free political prisoners living all around the world. Send for this "youth action pack," and you'll receive a description of a young prisoner you can help, an address for you to send your letter, and instructions on how to write the letter.

Directions:	Write your name, address, and request on a postcard.
Write to:	Amnesty International Urgent Action Network P.O. Box 1270 Nederland, CO 80466-1270
Ask for:	Children's Urgent Action Pack

International Pen Friends

Here's your chance to make friends with someone from another country. International Pen Friends links up kids who live in different corners of the world but have common interests. Send for this application, which allows you to request a list of ten pen pals to whom you can write.

 INTERNATIONAL PEN FRIENDS

Directions:	Write your request on paper and put it in an envelope. You must enclose a **long self-addressed, stamped envelope.**
Write to:	International Pen Friends Department FS6 1308 68th Lane North Brooklyn Center, MN 55430
Ask for:	IPF application and information

COLLECTIBLES

Flag Stickers

These colorful stickers feature the flags of ten different countries around the world. They're great for decorating your Social Studies or Geography notebook. You'll receive flag stickers of Hong Kong, Mexico, Great Britain, and others.

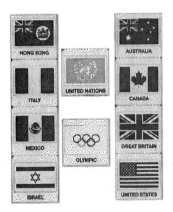

Directions:	Write your request on paper and put it in an envelope. You must enclose a **long self-addressed, stamped envelope** and **50¢**.
Write to:	Mr. Rainbows Department FS-11 P.O. Box 908 Rio Grande, NJ 08242
Ask for:	International flag stickers

Flag Decals

You name the country, and you'll receive one of these handsome decals featuring that country's flag. Choose any major country, including Brazil, Israel, England, and many others. Limit one country per request.

Directions:	Write your request on paper and put it in an envelope. You must enclose a **long self-addressed, stamped envelope** and **$1.00**.
Write to:	Parker Flags and Pennants Department 5 5750 Plunkett Street Hollywood, FL 33023
Ask for:	International flag decal *(You must specify the country you want.)*

Map Magnets

Here's a great way to learn geography and start a collection at the same time. These magnets outline the shapes of various countries and continents. You can choose from five different magnets: Australia, Mexico, Canada, Africa, or Puerto Rico. Limit one magnet per request.

Directions:	Write your request on paper and put it in an envelope. You must enclose **$1.00.**
Write to:	Special Products 34 Romeyn Avenue Department CM Amsterdam, NY 12010
Ask for:	• Australia map magnet **or** • Mexico map magnet **or** • Canada map magnet **or** • Africa map magnet **or** • Puerto Rico map magnet

Foreign Stamp Magnet

Now you can see what stamps from other countries look like! These fun magnets feature colorful foreign stamps, and they have your favorite Disney characters on them, too!

Directions:	Write your request on paper and put it in an envelope. You must enclose **75¢.**
Write to:	Hicks Specialties Department FS6 1308 68th Lane North Brooklyn Center, MN 55430
Ask for:	Disney stamp magnet

Jordan

Jordan is a country of great natural beauty, history, and culture. If you're studying the Middle East and want to learn more about it, send for this informational material about Jordan. It's great for school reports!

Directions:	Write your name, address, and request on a postcard.
Write to:	Jordan Information Bureau 2319 Wyoming Avenue NW Washington, DC 20008
Ask for:	Facts and Figures pamphlet

Austria

Learn all about Austria, a neighbor of Switzerland and Germany, with these materials from the Austrian National Tourist Office. You'll find out about Austria's cities, culture, and music, as well as the mighty Austrian Alps.

Directions:	Write your name, address, and request on a postcard.
Write to:	Austrian National Tourist Office Kids Department P.O. Box 1142 New York, NY 10108-1142
Ask for:	Tourist information packet

To receive free tourist information on foreign countries, send a postcard with your name, address, and request to the following addresses. (For those countries with more than one address, send your request to the one closest to your home.)

Barbados
Barbados Tourism Authority
800 Second Avenue, 2nd Floor
New York, NY 10017

Belgium
Belgium Tourist Office
780 Third Avenue, Suite 1501
New York, NY 10017

Côte D'Ivoire (Ivory Coast, Africa)
Tourisme Côte D'Ivoire
2424 Massachusetts Avenue NW
Washington, DC 22008

Cyprus
Cyprus Tourist Organization
13 East 40th Street
New York, NY 10016

Denmark
Danish Tourist Board
655 Third Avenue
New York, NY 10017

Egypt
Egyptian Tourist Authority
630 Fifth Avenue, Suite 1706
New York, NY 10111

Egyptian Tourist Authority
645 North Michigan Avenue, Suite 829
Chicago, IL 60611

Egyptian Tourist Authority
8383 Wilshire Boulevard, Suite 215
Beverly Hills, CA 90211

Finland
Finnish Tourist Board
655 Third Avenue
New York, NY 10017

France
French Government Tourist Office
444 Madison Avenue, 16th Floor
New York, NY 10022

French Government Tourist Office
676 North Michigan Avenue, Suite 3360
Chicago, IL 60611-2836

French Government Tourist Office
9454 Wilshire Boulevard, Suite 715
Beverly Hills, CA 90212-2967

Germany
German National Tourist Office
122 East 42nd Street, 52nd Floor
New York, NY 10168

Greece
Greek National Tourist Organization
645 Fifth Avenue
New York, NY 10022

Greek National Tourist Organization
168 North Michigan Avenue, Suite 600
Chicago, IL 60601

Greek National Tourist Organization
611 West 6th Street, Suite 2198
Los Angeles, CA 90017

OTHER COUNTRIES

Iceland
Iceland Tourist Board
655 Third Avenue
New York, NY 10017

Ireland
Irish Tourist Board
345 Park Avenue
New York, NY 10154

Japan
Japan National Tourist Organization
401 North Michigan Avenue, Suite 770
Chicago, IL 60611

Japan National Tourist Organization
Rockefeller Plaza
630 Fifth Avenue
New York, NY 10111

Japan National Tourist Organization
360 Post Street, Suite 601
San Francisco, CA 94108

Japan National Tourist Organization
624 South Grand Avenue, Suite 1611
Los Angeles, CA 90017

Kenya
Kenya Tourist Office
424 Madison Avenue
New York, NY 10017

Netherlands
Netherlands Board of Tourism
225 North Michigan Avenue, Suite 326
Chicago, IL 60601

Norway
Norwegian Information Service
825 Third Avenue, 38th Floor
New York, NY 10022

Portugal
Portuguese National Tourism Office
590 Fifth Avenue, 4th Floor
New York, NY 10036

Spain
Spanish National Tourist Office
665 Fifth Avenue
New York, NY 10022

Spanish National Tourist Office
1221 Brickell Avenue, Suite 1850
Miami, FL 33131

Spanish National Tourist Office
845 North Michigan Avenue
Chicago, IL 60611

Spanish National Tourist Office
8383 Wilshire Boulevard, Suite 960
Beverly Hills, CA 90211

Sweden
Swedish Tourist Board
655 Third Avenue
New York, NY 10017

Turkey
Turkish Culture and Tourism Office
1717 Massachusetts Avenue NW, Suite 306
Washington, DC 20036

Spanish Language

¿Quieres aprender español? That means "Do you want to learn Spanish?" If you do, send for this newsletter that will help you learn the meanings and pronunciations of some Spanish words. It even includes a word game and a special recipe in both Spanish and English.

Directions:	Write your request on paper and put it in an envelope. You must enclose **$1.00.**
Write to:	In One Ear Publications Suite F6 29481 Manzanita Drive Campo, CA 91906-1128
Ask for:	Bueno newsletter

Flag Pin

These metal pins of flags from countries around the world will look attractive on your hat or jacket, or will make a fine addition to your collection. You will receive a pin randomly selected from countries that include France, Canada, Great Britain, and others.

Directions:	Write your request on paper and put it in an envelope. You must enclose a **long self-addressed, stamped envelope** and **25¢.**
Write to:	Phyllis Goodstein Department FP P.O. Box 912 Levittown, NY 11756-0912
Ask for:	Flag pin

MEADOWBROOK PRESS
1996
EDITION

U.S.
MAIL

PETS AND ANIMALS

Dog Training Pamphlet

Is your family getting a new dog or puppy? Every new dog needs some training, and this pamphlet will teach you some simple techniques. You'll learn how to housebreak your dog and how to make it follow simple commands like sitting, staying, and lying down.

Directions:	Write your request on paper and put it in an envelope. You must enclose a **long self-addressed, stamped envelope.**
Write to:	Lawson and Lawson P.O. Box 32234 San Jose, CA 95152
Ask for:	Dog school pamphlet

Dog Care Tips

Knowing how to take care of a new dog or puppy is very important for keeping it healthy and happy. Get some tips on proper dog care, learn about the history of dogs, and check out a list of recommended books with this flyer from the American Society for the Prevention of Cruelty to Animals (ASPCA).

Directions:	Write your request on paper and put it in an envelope. You must enclose a **long self-addressed, stamped envelope.**
Write to:	Education Department ASPCA 424 East 92nd Street New York, NY 10128
Ask for:	Dog care tips

Dog Owner's Bookmark

Here's a great way to remind yourself how to be a responsible dog owner. This bookmark features Corey, the children's education mascot for the American Kennel Club. On the front, you'll find a handy "Responsible Dog Owner's Checklist."

Directions:	Write your request on paper and put it in an envelope. You must enclose a **long self-addressed, stamped envelope.**
Write to:	The American Kennel Club Public Education Department 51 Madison Avenue New York, NY 10010
Ask for:	Corey bookmark

Dog Storybook

This fun, ten-page storybook tells the story of Hope, a dog abandoned at an animal shelter with her three puppies. After reading it, you'll understand why every dog needs a loving owner. Choose one of two age levels.

Directions:	Write your request on paper and put it in an envelope. You must enclose a **long self-addressed, stamped envelope** and **two first-class stamps.**
Write to:	The Fund for Animals 808 Alamo Drive, Suite 306 Vacaville, CA 95688
Ask for:	• Dog coloring storybook (Grades K–2) **or** • Dog storybook (Grades 3–5)

Catnip

This offer will drive your cat wild with joy! An informational flyer explains the effects of catnip and how to give it to your cat responsibly. Plus, you'll get a generous packet of pure, premium catnip for your furry friend to enjoy.

Directions:	Write your request on paper and put it in an envelope. You must enclose a **long self-addressed, stamped envelope** and **$1.00.**
Write to:	Mountain Lion Catnip Department K P.O. Box 120 Forest Hill, WV 24935
Ask for:	Informational flyer and packet of catnip

Cat Care Tips

Learn all about cats and cat care with this flyer from the ASPCA. You'll get information on the history of cats, tips on how to take care of your cat, and a reading list of recommended books.

Directions:	Write your request on paper and put it in an envelope. You must enclose a **long self-addressed, stamped envelope.**
Write to:	Education Department ASPCA 424 East 92nd Street New York, NY 10128
Ask for:	Cat care tips

Proper Pet Care

Taking your pet to a veterinarian is just as important as your visiting a doctor. This offer features a brochure that tells you what a veterinary exam is all about and why it's important. You'll also get a sticker with a cat, dog, and bird on it to show that you're a kid who cares about pets.

Directions:	Write your request on paper and put it in an envelope. You must enclose a **long self-addressed, stamped envelope.**
Write to:	Attention: MSC American Animal Hospital P.O. Box 150899 Denver, CO 80125-0899
Ask for:	Health exam brochure and caring kids sticker

Pet Reading List

The members of Delta Society believe animals improve the lives and well-being of people. They also believe people can improve the lives and well-being of animals. To learn how, send for their list of books on human-animal relationships.

Directions:	Write your request on paper and put it in an envelope. You must enclose a **long self-addressed, stamped envelope.**
Write to:	DELTA SOCIETY P.O. Box 1080 Renton, WA 98057-9601
Ask for:	Free materials for kids

Zoo Animals

Learn all about three of the most popular zoo animals by sending for these informational pamphlets from the Cincinnati Zoo. The flyers are perfect for school reports. They describe the animals' daily habits, food, and areas where they live. You must specify which animal you want to learn about: Bengal tigers, Komodo dragons, or gorillas.

Directions:	Write your request on paper and put it in an envelope. You must enclose a **long self-addressed, stamped envelope.**
Write to:	Education Department Cincinnati Zoo P.O. Box 198073 Cincinnati, OH 45219-8073
Ask for:	• Bengal tiger pamphlet **or** • Komodo dragon pamphlet **or** • Gorilla pamphlet

Saddlebred Horses

The high-stepping Saddlebreds, known for their grace and personality, gained fame during the Civil War when they served as mounts for generals like Lee and Grant. This offer features a coloring poster, logo sticker, and informative brochures.

Directions:	Write your request on paper and put it in an envelope. You must enclose **$1.00.**
Write to:	ASHA Department S 4093 Iron Works Pike Lexington, KY 40511-8434
Ask for:	Coloring poster, sticker, and brochures

"Paws Off" Stickers

Mark your territory with these fun "Paws Off" stickers. You'll get twenty stickers perfect for labeling lunch boxes, lockers, or books. Each one features a place for your name and a colorful design of a wild animal. You'll also receive a "Wild Animals of the Safari" fact sheet telling you all about zebras, lions, and other animals.

Directions:	Write your request on paper and put it in an envelope. You must enclose **$1.00.**
Write to:	ITG Paws Off Stickers Department B P.O. Box 322 Munroe Falls, OH 44262
Ask for:	Paws Off stickers and safari fact sheet

Animal Booklet

Send for this colorful booklet from the American Society for the Prevention of Cruelty to Animals (ASPCA). You'll receive a random edition of their special kids publication "Eye on Animals." Find out about popular animals, pick up some good pet care tips, and learn responsible ways to treat animals with respect.

Directions:	Write your request on paper and put it in an envelope. You must enclose a **long self-addressed, stamped envelope.**
Write to:	Education Department ASPCA 424 East 92nd Street New York, NY 10128
Ask for:	Eye on Animals booklet

MEADOWBROOK PRESS
1996 EDITION

U.S. MAIL

ACTIVITIES AND COLLECTIONS

Footbag Sticker

Footbag is fun! Learn all about this great sport by sending for an official player's manual from the World Footbag Association. You'll get tips on the basics of the sport, a form you can use to join their organization, and a way-cool footbag sticker.

Directions:	Write your request on paper and put it in an envelope. You must enclose a **long self-addressed, stamped envelope.**
Write to:	World Footbag Association 1317 Washington Avenue Suite 7 Golden, CO 80401
Ask for:	Official player's manual and way-cool sticker

Roller Skating Sticker

Are you a roller skating fan? Send for this high-quality, embroidered sticker featuring a roller skate. It's perfect to stick on your skates or your school notebooks.

Directions:	Write your request on paper and put it in an envelope. You must enclose a **long self-addressed, stamped envelope** and **50¢.**
Write to:	Roller Skating Associations 7301 Georgetown Road Suite 123 Indianapolis, IN 46268 ATTN: Accounting
Ask for:	Roller skating sticker

Fishing Decal

If you love fishing, you'll love this decal, too. It says, "Get hooked on fishing, not drugs." Stick it on your tackle box and let everyone know you enjoy drug-free activities.

Directions:	Write your request on paper and put it in an envelope. You must enclose a **long self-addressed, stamped envelope.**
Write to:	Future Fisherman Foundation Department: Decal 1033 North Fairfax Street Suite 200 Alexandria, VA 22314
Ask for:	Hooked on Fishing decal

Mountain Biking

Mountain biking is a great way to have fun and exercise at the same time. This pamphlet from the International Mountain Biking Association (IMBA) will teach you a few simple safety rules. You'll also receive an IMBA sticker.

International Mountain Bicycling Association

Directions:	Write your request on paper and put it in an envelope. You must enclose a **long self-addressed, stamped envelope** and **25¢.**
Write to:	IMBA P.O. Box 7578 Boulder, CO 80306
Ask for:	Wild Willy pamphlet and IMBA sticker

Soap Box Derbies

On your mark, get set, go! Learn all about a classic American activity—soap box derbies. The latest Official All-American Soap Box Derby Activities Book describes everything you need to know about derbies and how to enter them.

Directions:	Write your name, address, and request on a postcard.
Write to:	All-American Soap Box Derby Department FSK P.O. Box 7233 Akron, OH 44306
Ask for:	The Official All-American Soap Box Derby Activities Book

Bowling Tips

Do you know how to pick out a bowling ball according to your weight, or how to take a four-step approach? This brochure will give you these tips on bowling, and many others!

Directions:	Write your request on paper and put it in an envelope. You must enclose a **long self-addressed, stamped envelope.**
Write to:	Young American Bowling Alliance 5301 South 76th Street Greendale, WI 53129
Ask for:	Bif's Fun-Damentals of Bowling brochure

ACTIVITIES

Horseshoe Pitching

Horseshoes aren't just for horses and good luck. Learn how to "throw a ringer" with this instructional pamphlet. It explains the rules and scoring of horseshoe pitching.

Directions:	Write your request on paper and put it in an envelope. You must enclose a **long self-addressed, stamped envelope.**
Write to:	NHPA Rural Route 2, Box 178 LaMonte, MO 65337
Ask for:	Rules of Horseshoe Pitching pamphlet

Model Railroads

Building model railroads and trains is lots of fun—especially because you're making something that moves! This colorful, photo-filled booklet shows you what this unique hobby is all about.

Directions:	Write your name, address, and request on a postcard.
Write to:	Kalmbach Publishing 21027 Crossroads Circle P.O. Box 1612 Waukesha, WI 53187
Ask for:	Your Introduction to Model Railroading booklet

Water Skiing Safety

Giving the thumbs-down sign when you're water skiing doesn't mean you're not having a good time—it signals the driver to slow down. Learn more about proper signaling and safety from this brochure.

Directions:	Write your request on paper and put it in an envelope. You must enclose a **long self-addressed, stamped envelope.**
Write to:	American Water Ski Association Department: Requests 799 Overlook Drive Winter Haven, FL 33884
Ask for:	Tips for Safe Water Skiing

Hiking Safety

Do you like adventures? Hiking is a great way to explore nature, exercise, and have lots of fun. This pamphlet is full of tips and safety reminders.

Directions:	Write your request on paper and put it in an envelope. You must enclose a **long, self-addressed stamped envelope.**
Write to:	American Hiking Society P.O. Box 20160 Washington, DC 22041-2160
Ask for:	Hiking Safety pamphlet

Canoeing Tips

Can you canoe? Before you try, you must learn how to get the canoe in the water, paddle, and stay safe as you move. This pamphlet welcomes you to the world of canoeing with lots of tips and safety reminders.

UNITED STATES CANOE

· U · S · C · A ·

ASSOCIATION, INC.

Directions:	Write your request on paper and put it in an envelope. You must enclose a **long self-addressed, stamped envelope.**
Write to:	United States Canoe Association 606 Ross Street Middletown, OH 45044-5062 ATTN: Jim Mack
Ask for:	Welcome Paddler! pamphlet

Dream Catcher Kit

In Native American lore, dream catchers are made to prevent nightmares from falling from the sky in the middle of the night. The bad dreams are caught in the web, while the good ones pass through. Make your own dream catcher to hang above your bed with this complete kit.

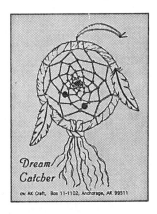

Dream Catcher

cw AK Craft, Box 11-1102, Anchorage, AK 99511

Directions:	Write your request on paper and put it in an envelope. You must enclose **$1.00.**
Write to:	Alaska Craft Department DC P.O. Box 11-1102 Anchorage, AK 99511-1102
Ask for:	Dream catcher kit and instructions

Assorted Milkcaps

It's a fad that's swept the nation! Starting in Hawaii, the milkcap craze has spread to the rest of the country and has become the most popular kids' game since marbles. Add twelve colorful caps featuring clowns, animals, and cartoon characters to your collection.

Peanuts Milkcaps

These milkcaps will be your favorites. You'll receive a total of ten milkcaps, two of which feature Snoopy, Charlie Brown, and other characters from the comic strip "Peanuts."

Directions:	Write your request on paper and put it in an envelope. You must enclose a **long self-addressed, stamped envelope** and **$1.00**.
Write to:	J.A. Williams P.O. Box 070914 Brooklyn, NY 11207
Ask for:	Free Stuff for Kids milkcap offer

Directions:	Write your request on paper and put it in an envelope. You must enclose a **long self-addressed, stamped envelope** and **$1.00**.
Write to:	Scana Enterprises P.O. Box 752084 Memphis, TN 38175-2084
Ask for:	Peanuts milkcap offer

Baseball Cards

Create an instant baseball card collection or add to one you already have with this great offer. You'll receive a packet of ten cards. Each one features a major league player, along with stats and batting averages on the back.

Dinosaur Trading Cards

Are you caught up in the dinosaur craze? Start a trading card collection with this colorful offer. You'll receive a set of three cards featuring pictures of your favorite dinosaurs. On the back of the cards you'll find statistics and descriptions for each dinosaur.

Directions:	Write your request on paper and put it in an envelope. You must enclose a **long self-addressed, stamped envelope** and **50¢.**
Write to:	DANORS Department C 5721 Funston Street, Bay 14 Hollywood, FL 33023
Ask for:	10 baseball cards

Directions:	Write your request on paper and put it in an envelope. You must enclose a **long self-addressed, stamped envelope** and **25¢** for **each** set of cards.
Write to:	SAV-ON P.O. Box 1356 Department DTC Gwinn, MI 49841
Ask for:	Dinosaur trading cards

Trolls

Here's your chance to have your own crazy-haired troll! Send for a loveable troll miniature to keep you smiling, or to give to a friend. You can choose from a troll key chain, pin, or pendant.

Directions:	Write your request on paper and put it in an envelope. You must enclose **50¢** for **each** troll you request.
Write to:	Surprise Gift of the Month Club Department: Trolls P.O. Box 1 Stony Point, NY 10980
Ask for:	• Troll key chain **or** • Troll pin **or** • Troll pendant

Funny Money

These replicas of U.S. money are great for playing games and trading. You'll receive a packet of three different types of bills: jumbo size, half size, and micro size.

Directions:	Write your request on paper and put it in an envelope. You must enclose a **long self-addressed, stamped envelope** and **50¢**.
Write to:	DANORS Department M 5721 Funston Street, Bay 14 Hollywood, FL 33023
Ask for:	Funny money

Dollhouse Miniatures

This hobby embraces both collecting and crafting. Discover how much fun miniatures can be with this booklet, which describes everything you need to know about both collecting and assembling dollhouse miniatures.

Directions:	Write your name, address, and request on a postcard.
Write to:	Kalmbach Publishing Co. 21027 Crossroads Circle P.O. Box 1612 Waukesha, WI 53187
Ask for:	Discovering Miniatures booklet

Sports Pins

Are you a pin collector? Decorate your favorite hat or jacket with these high-quality enamel sports pins. You can choose from four designs, including football, baseball, basketball, and soccer ball.

Directions:	Write your request on paper and put it in an envelope. You must enclose a **long self-addressed, stamped envelope** and **50¢** for **each** pin you request.
Write to:	Surprise Gift of the Month Club Department SPPN P.O. Box 1 Stony Point, NY 10980
Ask for:	• Football pin **or** • Baseball pin **or** • Basketball pin **or** • Soccer ball pin

Tanagram Puzzle

Tanagram puzzles were invented in China centuries ago. They have challenged and entertained many people throughout history, including famous people like Edgar Allan Poe and Napoleon. You'll receive a complete, seven-piece puzzle set and directions.

Directions:	Write your request on paper and put it in an envelope. You must enclose **50¢.**
Write to:	Alaska Craft Department TG P.O. Box 11-1102 Anchorage, AK 99511-1102
Ask for:	Tanagram puzzle

Bunny Trail Game

Here's a great game to chase away the rainy-day blues. The object of the Bunny Trail game is to hop your bunny all the way around the board before anyone else can. You'll receive a complete game, including board, pieces, and instructions on how to play.

Directions:	Write your request on paper and put it in an envelope. You must enclose **$1.00.**
Write to:	Joan Nykorchuk 13236 North 7th Street, #4 Suite 237 Phoenix, AZ 85022
Ask for:	Bunny Trail game

AWARENESS AND SELF-ESTEEM

Friendship Tips Flyer

We all know people we would like to become friends with, but sometimes it's hard to make friends. This flyer offers advice on what to do when you meet someone you'd like to know better, as well as how you can make friends with children with disabilities. You'll also receive a button with this friendship symbol on it.

Directions:	Write your request on paper and put it in an envelope. You must enclose a **long self-addressed, stamped envelope.**
Write to:	Beach Center on Families and Disability University of Kansas 3111 Haworth Hall Lawrence, KS 66045
Ask for:	Friendship flyer and button

Pen Pal Club

Meet new people and learn about other parts of the United States without leaving your house! With a pen pal, you can share information about your family, school, and neighborhood. You'll receive a list of pen pals with similar interests as yours, plus this fun "Friendship Club" button.

Directions:	Write your request on paper and put it in an envelope. You must enclose a **long self-addressed, stamped envelope** and **60¢.**
Write to:	E. Williams P.O. Box 914 Brooklyn, NY 11207-0914
Ask for:	Friendship Club button and pen pals *(You must list your age, grade, and favorite activities.)*

Friendship Bracelets

Add meaning to your friendships by sending for these colorful bracelets. You'll receive a red, a white, and a blue bracelet. Keep one for yourself and share the others with two of your best friends!

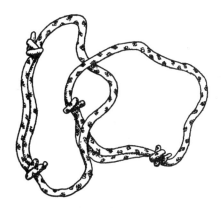

Directions:	Write your request on paper and put it in an envelope. You must enclose a **long self-addressed, stamped envelope** and **50¢.**
Write to:	Fax Marketing 460-B Carrollton Drive Frederick, MD 21701-6357
Ask for:	Red, white, and blue friendship bracelets

Best Friend Necklaces

These two necklaces are perfect for you and your best friend. Each necklace features half a heart. When you put them together you'll make a whole heart that says "Best Friend."

Directions:	Write your request on paper and put it in an envelope. You must enclose **$1.00.**
Write to:	Lightning Enterprises P.O. Box 16121 West Palm Beach, FL 33416
Ask for:	Best friend necklaces

Friendship Credit Card

Here's a fun way to say "thanks for being a great friend" to someone special. You'll receive a small "credit card" that comes in its own envelope. The card tells your friend that he or she "deserves credit" for being the greatest in the world.

Directions:	Write your request on paper and put it in an envelope. You must enclose a **long self-addressed, stamped envelope** and **$1.00**.
Write to:	Marlene Monroe Department FC 6210 Ridge Manor Drive Memphis, TN 38115-3411
Ask for:	Friendship credit card

Big Brothers/Big Sisters

Big Brothers/Big Sisters is an organization that matches up children with adult friends. Find out more about what they do with this informational pamphlet called "Help Them Grow into Their Dreams."

Directions:	Write your request on paper and put it in an envelope. You must enclose a **long self-addressed, stamped envelope**.
Write to:	Big Brothers/Big Sisters of America Marketing and Communications 230 North 13th Street Philadelphia, PA 19107
Ask for:	Help Them Grow into Their Dreams pamphlet

Special Olympics

Special Olympics celebrates the athletic achievements of people with mental retardation. Their free materials tell you how their program works, and how you can get involved as a volunteer.

Special Olympics
International

Directions:	Write your name, address, and request on a postcard.
Write to:	Special Olympics International c/o Free Stuff for Kids 1325 G Street NW Suite 500 Washington, DC 20005
Ask for:	Free information for kids

Learn about Stuttering

Stuttering is a speech problem that affects twenty-five percent of kids at one time or another. Pick up some more facts about this issue and learn about ways to deal with stuttering by sending for one or more of these pamphlets.

STUTTERING
FOUNDATION
OF AMERICA

Directions:	Write your name, address, and request on a postcard. *Or call 1-800-992-9392.*
Write to:	Stuttering Foundation of America Department FS 3100 Walnut Grove Road, #603 Memphis, TN 38111
Ask for:	• Did You Know? fact sheet **or** • How to React When Speaking with Someone Who Stutters fact sheet **or** • The Child Who Stutters at School: Notes to the Teacher pamphlet **or** • If You Think Your Child Is Stuttering pamphlet

Sign Language

Did you know that sign language is the third most popular language in the United States? Here's a great way to learn some sign language. You'll receive a poster and three postcards that teach you how to make signs for the letters in the alphabet. Soon you'll be speaking without a sound!

Directions:	Write your request on paper and put it in an envelope. You must enclose a **long self-addressed, stamped envelope** and **$1.00.**
Write to:	Keep Quiet P.O. Box 367 Stanhope, NJ 07874
Ask for:	Poster and postcard offer

Join SADD

SADD (Students Against Driving Drunk) works to prevent death and injury from underage drinking and driving and drug use. Find out more about their efforts by sending for an informational pamphlet. You'll also receive a "Contract for Life," which you and your parents can discuss and sign.

Directions:	Write your request on paper and put it in an envelope. You must enclose a **long self-addressed, stamped envelope.**
Write to:	SADD P.O. Box 800 Marlboro, MA 01752
Ask for:	SADD pamphlet and Contract for Life

Operation Lifesaver

Operation Lifesaver wants you to stay safe and sound. Their coloring and activity book will show you how to keep out of danger when playing or walking near railroad tracks. You can also receive a bookmark that reminds you to "Look, Listen . . . and Live." Limit one item per request.

Directions:	Write your name, address, and request on a postcard.
Write to:	Operation Lifesaver 1420 King Street, Suite 401 Alexandria, VA 22314
Ask for:	• Coloring/activity book or • Bookmark

Fitness Awards

The President wants to help you get physically **fit!** Take the Presidential Sports Award challenge **by** participating in sports ranging from football **to** ice-skating. Find out about all the cool awards **you can** receive with this pamphlet.

Directions:	Write your request on paper and put it in an envelope. You must enclose a **long self-addressed, stamped envelope.**
Write to:	Presidential Sports Award P.O. Box 68207 Indianapolis, IN 46268-0207
Ask for:	Presidential Sports Award pamphlet

Self-Esteem Stickers

Show the world that you know you're special. These stickers say things like "I Like Being Me" and "It Feels Good to Be Me." Others warn about staying away from drugs. You'll receive two sheets.

Directions:	Write your request on paper and put it in an envelope. You must enclose **$1.00.** *No checks please.*
Write to:	Safe Child P.O. Box 40-1594 Brooklyn, NY 11240-1594
Ask for:	Self-esteem stickers

Girls Growing Up

Growing up is serious business, and you might have questions about the changes you're going through. This eight-page booklet for girls, featuring the cartoon character Luann, is filled with comic strips and useful information about becoming a teenager.

Directions:	Write your request on paper and put it in an envelope. You must enclose **$1.00.**
Write to:	Girls Incorporated National Resource Center Department: Luann 441 West Michigan Street Indianapolis, IN 46202
Ask for:	Luann Becomes a Woman booklet

Your Birthday's History

Find out about the history of your birthday. This fact sheet tells you what special events happened the day and year you were born. You'll learn which famous people share your birthday, what the top songs and movies were, and more!

Directions:	Write your request on paper and put it in an envelope. You must enclose a **long self-addressed, stamped envelope** and **$1.00.**
Write to:	Special Products Department FS-1 P.O. Box 6605 Delray Beach, FL 33482-6605
Ask for:	Happy Birthday sheet *(You must include the date, month, and year of your birth and the state in which you were born.)*

Modeling

Did you ever wish to be a preteen or teen model? If so, send for your free Barbizon modeling newsletter, which talks about this challenging profession and how it can help develop your poise and confidence.

Directions:	Write your name, address, and request on a postcard.
Write to:	Barbizon Information Center Department FK 2240 Woolbright Road Boynton Beach, FL 33426
Ask for:	Modeling newsletter

Feeling Special

Whether you're a boy or girl, black or white, tall or short, you are a special person. Inside this coloring book, you'll find lots of activities that remind you to give yourself credit and teach you how to gain self-esteem.

Directions:	Write your request on paper and put it in an envelope. You must enclose **$1.00** and **one first-class stamp.** *No checks please.*
Write to:	Safe Child P.O. Box 40-1594 Brooklyn, NY 11240-1594
Ask for:	You Are Special coloring book

Having Pride

It's important to believe in the things you do and to learn how to take pride in your achievements. This coloring and activity book teaches you about having pride and believing in yourself.

Directions:	Write your request on paper and put it in an envelope. You must enclose **$1.00** and **one first-class stamp.** *No checks please.*
Write to:	Safe Child P.O. Box 40-1594 Brooklyn, NY 11240-1594
Ask for:	Proud to Be Me coloring book

INDEX

INDEX

MORE BOOKS KIDS WILL LOVE!

A Bad Case of the Giggles
selected by Bruce Lansky
illustrated by Stephen Carpenter

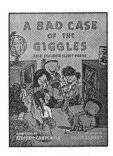

Nothing motivates your children to read more than a book that makes them laugh. That's why this book will turn your kids into poetry lovers. Every poem included in this book had to pass the giggle test of over 600 school children. This anthology collects the royal court of children's poets (court jesters all), Shel Silverstein, Jack Prelutsky, Judith Viorst, Jeff Moss, and Bruce Lansky. The American Booksellers Association has chosen this book as "Pick of the Lists" for children's poetry.   **order #2411**

Kids Pick the Funniest Poems
compiled by Bruce Lansky
illustrated by Stephen Carpenter

Three hundred elementary kids will tell you that this book contains the funniest poems for kids—because they picked them! Not surprisingly, they chose many of the funniest poems ever written by favorites like Shel Silverstein, Jack Prelutsky, Jeff Moss, and Judith Viorst (plus poems by lesser-known writers that are just as funny). This book is guaranteed to please children aged 6–12!   **order #2410**

Girls to the Rescue
selected by Bruce Lansky

A collection of 10 folk and fairy tales featuring courageous, clever, and determined girls from around the world. This groundbreaking book will update traditional fairy tales for girls aged 8–12.   **order #2215**

*"An enjoyable, much-needed addition to children's literature
that portrays female characters in positive, active roles."*
                    —Colleen O'Shaughnessy McKenna, author of
                    Too Many Murphys

Order Form

Quantity	Title	Author	Order No.	Unit Cost	Total
	A Bad Case of the Giggles	Lansky, Bruce	2411	$14.00	
	Dads Say the Dumbest Things!	Lansky/Jones	4220	$6.00	
	Dino Dots	Dixon, Dougal	2250	$4.95	
	Free Stuff for Kids, 1996 edition	Free Stuff Editors	2190	$5.00	
	Funny Side of Parenthood	Lansky, Bruce	4015	$6.00	
	Girls to the Rescue	Lansky, Bruce	2215	$3.95	
	Grandma Knows Best	McBride, Mary	4009	$6.00	
	Kids' Holiday Fun	Warner, Penny	6000	$12.00	
	Kids' Party Games and Activities	Warner, Penny	6095	$12.00	
	Kids Pick the Funniest Poems	Lansky, Bruce	2410	$14.00	
	Learn While You Scrub, Science in the Tub	Lewis, James	2350	$7.00	
	Moms Say the Funniest Things!	Lansky, Bruce	4280	$6.00	
	New Adventures of Mother Goose	Lansky, Bruce	2420	$15.00	
	Webster's Dictionary Game	Webster, Wilbur	6030	$5.95	
				Subtotal	
			Shipping and Handling (see below)		
			MN residents add 6.5% sales tax		
				Total	

YES, please send me the books indicated above. Add $2.00 shipping and handling for the first book and $.50 for each additional book. Add $2.50 to total for books shipped to Canada. Overseas postage will be billed. Allow up to 4 weeks for delivery. Send **check** or money order payable to Meadowbrook Press. No cash or C.O.D.'s, please. Prices subject to change without notice. **Quantity discounts available upon request.**

Send book(s) to:

Name _____ Phone _____

Address _____

City_____ State_____ Zip_____

Payment via:

❏ Check or money order payable to Meadowbrook Press. (No cash or C.O.D.'s, please.) Amount enclosed $_____

❏ Visa (for orders over $10.00 only)   ❏ MasterCard (for orders over $10.00 only)

Account #_____ Signature_____ Exp. Date _____

A FREE Meadowbrook Press catalog is available upon request.
You can also phone us for orders of $10.00 or more at 1-800-338-2232.

Mail to: Meadowbrook, Inc., 18318 Minnetonka Blvd., Deephaven, MN 55391

(612) 473-5400   Toll-Free 1-800-338-2232   FAX (612) 475-0736